Tales from African Dreamtime

Retold by Magdalene Sacranie

Illustrated by Sarah Bramley

Floris Books

Illustrations by Sarah Bramley

Cover and endpaper illustrations by Tony Spearing

First published in 2009 by Floris Books
Text © 2009 Magdalene Sacranie

British Library CIP data available
ISBN 978-086315-676-2

Printed in Singapore

For Hamid

and

Sorcha & Aisha

and children everywhere

Contents

MOROCCO
ALGERIA
LIBYA
EGYPT
SENEGAL MALI
NIGER
CHAD
SUDAN
LIBERIA
GHANA NIGERIA
ETHIOPIA
CAMEROON
UGANDA
KENYA
CONGO
TANZANIA
ZAIRE
MALAWI
ZAMBIA
ANGOLA
ZIMBABWE
MOZAMBIQUE
MADAGASCAR
SOUTH AFRICA
SWAZILAND

Foreword

I first became interested in African folk tales in 1980, when I was living in Swaziland. I did not investigate the Swazi tradition, however — my interest centred on the folk tale tradition of the Ndbele people of southern Zimbabwe. Later I collected a number of folk tales from that group and was thoroughly taken with the freshness and beauty of many of these stories.

Like all folk tales, there is often a moral lurking in the African traditional story. Virtue is rewarded; dishonesty punished; selfishness shown for what it is. The values that one can detect in these African stories are the deep values of African societies, and in reading these stories today we are given a glimpse of what it is that makes Sub-Saharan Africa so special.

In bringing these stories to a wider readership, Magdalene Sacranie is helping to further our understanding of Africa. Too often, the picture that we get of African countries is a bleak one, and we see little of the joy and humour which is so immediately and strikingly evident to any visitor to that part of the world.

Alexander McCall Smith

I have spread
my dreams
under your feet;
Tread softly
because you
tread on
my dreams.

W.B. Yeats

Introduction

For as long as people have lived together in groups, stories have been told to try and make sense of the mysteries of life. These folk tales, or wisdom stories, come from the depths of the collective psyche and are like a shared and familiar dream. The truths of these dreams serve to guide and teach us through life's stages and transitions, through good times and bad.

Wisdom stories were traditionally told by the elders of the group, and besides being a wonderful source of entertainment, they served to emphasise the consequences of certain behaviour. Universally popular and familiar themes include the triumph of good over evil, being patient and determined in the face of hardship, and being true to oneself.

Folk tales have been used all around the world throughout all civilizations in just this way, and have served as the building blocks for the early development of culture.

Tales from African Dreamtime is a collection of wisdom stories from several different African traditions. Like much-loved stories everywhere, they will bring enjoyment and satisfaction, and enlighten both reader and listener alike. With each telling of these magical tales, truths and meaning will resonate in different ways for people everywhere.

And so, whether you are reading to yourself or aloud to a group, receive the cloak of the Storyteller and let the tale tell itself! And if you are the Listener, one of the dear Brothers and Sisters, gather in, draw closer, and open your heart to the wisdom of these ancient stories.

How Wisdom Was Spread

A tale from Ghana

Long, long ago, dear Brothers and Sisters, when the World was still new, Kwaku Ananse the Spider was considered to be, and thought of himself it has to be said, the Wisest Person in all the Land

However, Kwaku Ananse was also very greedy and wished to keep all this Wisdom to himself. Day and night and night and day, Kwaku Ananse jealously guarded his Wisdom, until one day when he said to his wife, "It is too difficult for me to guard my Wisdom all the time. Make me a large clay pot into which I can put my Wisdom, and then I will put the pot in a safe place."

When the clay pot had baked hard in the hot sun, Kwaku Ananse took all his Wisdom, poured it into the pot and stopped up the hole with a piece of cork-wood.

Cunning Kwaku Ananse decided to hide his pot in a cave in the riverbank opposite his hut where no prying eyes would see it.

He lifted the pot with some difficulty and waded out into the water. Unfortunately, the stones on the riverbed were slippery and Kwaku Ananse the Spider felt his legs sliding under him.

As he fell into the water, the pot with all the Wisdom in the World went flying up into the air.

As the pot crashed down against the stones, it smashed into one hundred pieces and, Dear Ones, all the Wisdom in the World was washed away down the river.

The river, full of Wisdom, flowed on out to all the Great Seas, and that is how Wisdom was spread throughout the World.

God gives blessings to all men. If man had to distribute them, many would

go without.

Hausa

The Basket of Dreams

A story from South Africa

Come close to the fire, dear Brothers and Sisters, and I will tell you a tale.

Once upon a time and long ago, there lived a Herdsman far away out on the grasslands. He was all alone except for his cattle, which he loved dearly. Every morning he would rise before dawn to milk them, then he would take them out to graze, and at sunset he would bring them inside his *kraal* to keep them safe from leopards and hyenas prowling in the night.

One morning the Herdsman was surprised to find his cows empty of milk. He thought this very strange and took them to graze on lush long grass beside a stream.

The next morning the cows were once again dry.

The Herdsman was determined to find out the reason for this. After another day on the lush long grass he led his cattle back to the *kraal*, and then hid himself to keep watch over them.

Presently, a gap opened in the clouds that were sailing in the night sky and a shaft of moonlight shone down upon the sleeping cattle. Three women came walking down the moonbeam, their hips swaying, their skin shining, and each one carried on her head a giant calabash. The Herdsman was struck by their beauty.

When the women reached the ground they began to collect the milk from the cows in their calabashes. Suddenly the Herdsman came to his senses. The women were stealing his milk!

He jumped up and chased the women round and round. Two of them were too quick and escaped up the moonbeam with their full calabashes. The third woman was too slow, and the Herdsman captured her and held her fast until the moonbeam was gone.

The Herdsman was enchanted by her beauty and realized how lonely he had been, and so he asked her to stay with him and be his wife.

She replied that she would gladly be his wife, but first she had to return home to fetch her things.

This she did, returning the next evening,

again down the moonbeam, and carrying over her arm a basket with a lid. She told the Herdsman that she would be his wife, but that he must promise never to lift the lid and look inside her basket.

The Herdsman promised readily, and the two of them lived happily together as man and wife. Each day, while he watched the cattle, she would gather nuts, roots and herbs from the forest. Sometimes, after the evening meal the wife would lift the lid from her basket and gaze into it with such delight and rapture that the Herdsman felt very curious and not a little jealous. He longed to know what secrets were inside the basket.

One moonlit night, when his wife was late returning to the hut, the Herdsman could restrain himself no longer. He lifted the lid and saw to his surprise, and then anger, that the basket was empty! He realized that his wife had been testing him.

When she came back, she saw the basket and lid on the floor where the Herdsman had thrown them in his anger.

"You looked!" she said.

"Yes, I looked," the Herdsman shouted. "Why have you been playing this game with me when there was nothing in the basket?"

"You saw nothing?"

"It's empty," he repeated.

"Oh no," said the woman. "It's not empty. It's full of all my hopes and all my dreams, and in good time I would have shown you everything."

Sadly she picked up her basket and replaced the lid. Then she went outside. A shaft of moonlight was shining on the sleeping cattle.

The Herdsman watched as she stepped on to the moonbeam and climbed slowly up and up. She got smaller and smaller and then vanished through a gap in the clouds.

The Herdsman never saw her again.

How Tortoise Got His Shell

A story from Nigeria

Once upon a time, dear Brothers and Sisters, all the birds were invited to a Great Feast in the Sky.

They were very excited and began to prepare for the great day. They painted their bodies with red cam wood and drew beautiful patterns on themselves with *uli*.

Cunning Tortoise saw all the preparations and soon found out about the Great Feast in the Sky. Nothing in the World of Animals ever escaped his notice. His throat itched at the thought of the Great Feast. There was a famine in those days and Tortoise had not eaten for two moons. His body rattled like a dry stick in his shell. And so he began to plan how he also would go to the Great Feast in the Sky.

You are right, dear Brothers and Sisters, Tortoise had no wings! He went to the birds and asked to be allowed to go with them.

"We know you too well," replied the birds. "You are too full of cunning and you are ungrateful. If we allow you to come with us you will soon begin your mischief."

"You do not know me," said Tortoise. "I have had a change of heart. I have learnt that one who makes trouble for others ends in making the most trouble for himself."

Tortoise had such a sweet tongue that the birds all agreed he was a changed man. They each gave him a feather with which he made two wings.

At last the great day came and the birds flew off together with Tortoise in the middle.

Tortoise was very happy because not only had the birds allowed him to join them, they had also chosen him to speak for the party.

"There is one custom that we must not forget," he declared as they flew on their way. "When people are

invited to a great feast like this, they take new names for the occasion. Our hosts in the sky will expect us to honour this age-old tradition."

The birds had not heard of this custom, but respected Tortoise as a widely travelled man who knew the customs of different people, and they each took a new name. Tortoise also took one. He was to be called *All of You*.

At last the party arrived in the Sky and their hosts were very happy to see them.

Tortoise stood up in his many-coloured plumage and thanked them for their invitation. His speech was so eloquent that all the birds were glad they had brought him, and nodded their heads in approval of everything he said.

Their hosts took Tortoise to be King of the birds, especially as he looked somewhat different from the others.

After kola nuts had been presented and eaten, the people of the Sky set before their guests the most delectable dishes Tortoise had ever seen or dreamt of. Soup was brought out hot from the fire in the very pot it had been cooked in. It was full of delicious meat and fish. Tortoise began, rather rudely, dear Brothers and Sisters, to sniff aloud. There was pounded yam, yam pottage with palm oil and fresh fish. There were also pots of palm wine.

When everything had been set before the guests, one of the people of the Sky came forward and tasted a little from each pot. He then invited the birds to eat. But Tortoise jumped to his feet and asked, "For whom have you prepared this feast?"

"For all of you," replied the man.

Tortoise turned to the birds and said, "You remember that my name is *All of You*. The custom here is to serve the spokesman first and the others later. They will serve you when I have eaten."

He began to eat and the birds grumbled angrily. The people of the Sky thought it must be the birds' custom to leave all the food for their King. And so Tortoise ate the best part of the food and drank two pots of palm wine. He was so full of food and drink that his body filled out in his shell.

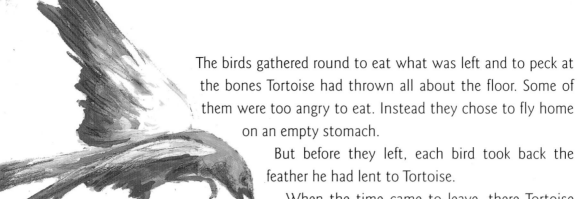

The birds gathered round to eat what was left and to peck at the bones Tortoise had thrown all about the floor. Some of them were too angry to eat. Instead they chose to fly home on an empty stomach.

But before they left, each bird took back the feather he had lent to Tortoise.

When the time came to leave, there Tortoise stood in his hard shell, full of food and wine but without any wings to fly home. He asked the birds to help him get home, but they all refused.

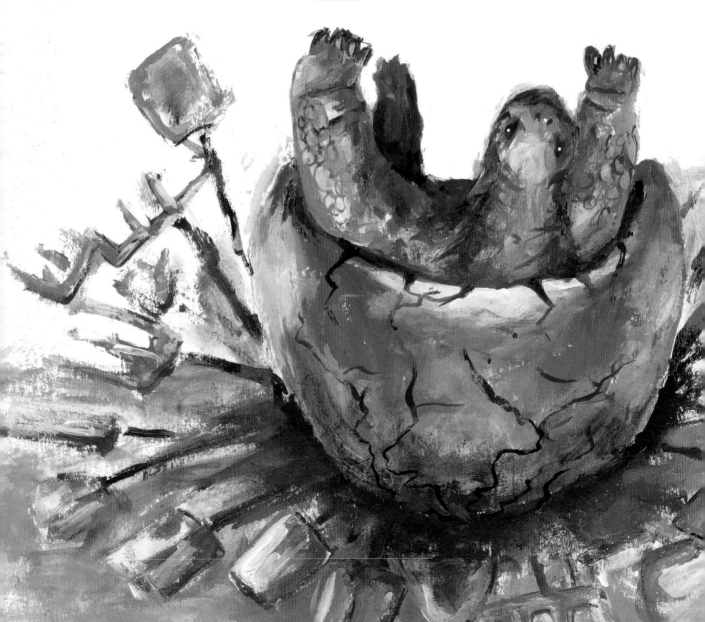

He begged the birds to take a message to his wife, but they all refused.

In the end, Parrot, who had felt angrier than the others, suddenly changed his mind and agreed to take the message.

"Tell my wife," said Tortoise, "to bring out all the soft things in my house and cover the compound with them so that I can jump down from the sky without great danger."

Parrot promised to deliver the message, and then flew away.

When Parrot reached Tortoise's house he told his wife to bring out all the *hard* things in the house. And so she brought out her husband's hoes, hatchets, spears, guns and even his cannon.

Tortoise looked down from the sky and saw his wife bringing things out, but it was too far to see what they were. When all seemed ready he let himself go. Tortoise fell and fell and fell until he began to fear that he would never stop falling.

And then, just like the sound of his cannon, he crashed into the compound.

Tortoise's shell shattered into many pieces. He was a broken man, but his good and generous wife took pity on him. Fortunately, there was a great medicine man in the neighbourhood. Tortoise's wife sent for him and together they gathered all the bits of shell and, taking great care, toiled for many hours until every piece of shell had been glued back into place.

Tortoise was much humbled by his experience and indeed became a changed man.

And that, dear Brothers and Sisters, is why Tortoise's shell is the way it is.

The Two Brothers

A story from Cameroon

Our story is of two brothers.

The younger brother was happy and hardworking and could buy all that was needed for himself and his merry young wife.

The elder brother had always been jealous of his younger brother's success.

At last, consumed by his own jealousy, he secretly planned to kill his younger brother, so that he could inherit his cattle, goats, garments and money.

It happened that one day the two brothers set out on a hunting trip.

The scheming older brother said to his younger brother, "Climb up those vines above the Hot Springs where the fruits are growing, and throw some down for me to eat."

The younger brother did as he was told.

After the older brother had had his fill, he reached for his machete and cut down the vines, leaving his brother suspended high up above the water.

The older brother then returned to the village, explaining that his brother was coming back another way.

But as time passed and the younger brother did not return, everyone agreed that he was lost for ever. As he had planned, the elder brother inherited all his brother's cattle, goats, garments and money.

All agreed, that is, except the younger brother's first wife. She faithfully searched day after day for her beloved husband. She went out into the forests where the vines grew thick and kept looking for her young husband.

One day, when she was out searching near the Hot Springs, her eye chanced on something hanging high up among the vines. As she drew closer, she recognised that it was her husband. But she did not know how she was going to get him down.

As she was trying to find a way to climb up the vines to rescue him, she happened to stub her toe on a magical root that told her what she must do.

Then marvellously the vine extended down towards her, carrying her husband, who she saw was now as thin as a chameleon.

The faithful wife picked up her husband and easily carried him home. When she got back, it was evening and already dark.

While the elder brother enjoyed the fruits of his younger brother's hard work and good nature, the good wife kept her husband hidden in her hut and secretly fed him to restore his health and strength. He began to put weight on and his stomach started to protrude a little again.

Soon the younger brother was well and once more a healthy and strong man. One day his wife revealed him to all the people in the village. Everyone was amazed and delighted to see the young man again. But they were so angry at the treachery of the older brother that he was banished from the village and was never seen again.

The Hunter, the Egg, the Broom and the Stone

(How man lost his tail)

A tale from the Congo

Long, long ago, dear Brothers and Sisters, in a time when Man and the Animals all spoke the same language, there lived a wise and elderly Chief who had a beautiful daughter. Many young men had sought the Chief's daughter's hand in marriage, but none had been successful.

Then one day, when the sun was high in the sky, there came a young Hunter to the Chief's compound, asking for his daughter's hand in marriage.

The young Hunter was so handsome and good that the Chief spoke to him kindly, "You may have my beautiful daughter for your wife, but first you must slay Ngaru Garu, the terrible monster that lives in the mountains far to the East and many days' journey from here."

The young Hunter agreed and set out on his journey.

He walked all day and the next day, even when the sun was at its highest point in the sky. On the third day he could see the mountains in the distance. On the fourth day he came across an old woman sitting under a shady tree.

"Have pity on me!" she cried as the young Hunter came near. "Take my calabash to the river and bring me water to drink."

Without any hesitation the young Hunter stopped to help the old woman and took her calabash to the river. As soon as he dipped the calabash into the water, it broke and out fell three things.

An egg, a broom made from fine palm fronds and a smooth round stone.

Then the old woman, who no longer appeared so ancient, said, "You are a brave and worthy Hunter. Take these three things, use them one by one in times of great danger."

The young Hunter thanked her and went on his way.

On the following day the young Hunter reached the mountains and started to climb through dense trees, thick undergrowth and trailing vines.

Suddenly he heard a great roaring sound and then the noise of a creature crashing through the jungle towards him. And there appeared Ngaru Garu, a terrible monster with two heads and fire pouring from his nostrils.

This must be the mountain monster!

The brave young Hunter took aim and shot his arrows, but these arrows could not stop Ngaru Garu, who tossed them aside like sticks.

Then the young Hunter set his dogs on the monster, but Ngaru Garu opened his enormous jaws and swallowed the dogs in one huge gulp.

Next, the young Hunter threw his spear with all his might. The spear broke in two when it struck Ngaru Garu, who roared even louder and leapt after the young Hunter.

This was now a time of grave danger, dear Brothers and Sisters, and our young Hunter turned round and just in time threw down the egg that the old woman had given him.

But not before the monster caught and wrenched away the young Hunter's tail!

As the egg struck the ground, a great lake appeared and the monster was forced to swim.

The young Hunter ran on as swiftly as the wind, but when he looked around he saw Ngaru Garu climbing out of the lake and almost catching up with him again.

Just in time the young Hunter threw down the broom, made from fine palm fronds, that the old woman had given him. As the broom struck the ground there sprung up a dense and dark forest.

The young Hunter ran on even more swiftly. But when he looked behind he saw Ngaru Garu crashing out of the forest and almost upon him for a third time!

Just in time, the young Hunter threw down the smooth round stone that the old woman had given him, and as the stone struck the ground there appeared the widest and highest mountain range that had ever been seen!

Now the young Hunter looked behind and could no longer see Ngaru Garu the mountain monster. So he returned triumphantly and with great joy to claim the Chief's beautiful daughter as his wife.

There was feasting and celebrating for many days and the drumming and dancing went on for many nights ... such was the people's rejoicing.

And to this day Ngaru Garu roars and roams about, lost in that mountain range.

And that is why, dear Brothers and Sisters, no Man since has ever had a tail.

The Bull and the Woman

A Bushman tale from South Africa

Long ago, dear Brothers and Sisters, at the beginning of time, when all things were new, Rain visited the Earth in the shape of a magnificent Bull to court and woo a beautiful young woman.

The Bull scented the fragrance of the woman from afar and, following the scent, found her resting in a shady grove.

The woman recognised that she had been royally summoned by the Bull and placed a garland of wild herbs on his head. Then she gently laid her sleeping baby down on the mossy ground so that she could tend to the Bull.

She climbed on to the broad back of the Bull and guided him to a shady tree in a deep ravine. Here the woman dismounted and soothed the Bull to sleep.

Later, when the Bull woke up, he rose up believing that the woman was still on his back.

Then, as Rain, the Bull returned to his own element in the water at the centre of a spring.

We remember this story whenever we see a fountain of clear water bubbling out of the Earth, and it reminds us to be thankful for Rain and to always welcome it.

The Lost Amulet

A Nyanja tale from Malawi

Long, long ago, dear Brothers and Sisters, when All Living Creatures could talk to each other, there lived a Chief who had a son called Ntagi.

Ntagi loved to swim in the river that flowed near his village, and all the Water Creatures that lived in the river were his friends.

One day, Ntagi dived from a high rock into the river. When he climbed out again he found that the precious Amulet that his father, the Chief, had hung around his neck, in order to protect him from all harm, was missing!

Ntagi called anxiously to all the Water Creatures, "Please help me to find my precious Amulet."

Immediately all his good friends the Water Creatures came and searched the river. They had to help Ntagi find his precious Amulet, before any harm came to their young friend!

Catfish searched under every stone.

Lake Salmon swam up and down looking in all the riverbank caves.

Crab hunted in every crevice.

Turtle scuttled back and forth across the riverbed.

And Minnow wove in amongst all the water-weeds looking everywhere.

Even Eel, who always swam alone, slithered and squeezed behind each and every rock, his bright eyes piercing the gloomy depths ...

But it was all in vain.

The precious Amulet was nowhere to be seen.

Just then, Mvu the River King came and listened to the story of the missing Amulet.

Mvu said, "One of you Water Creatures has taken Ntagi's precious Amulet." And in a commanding voice he asked, "Who is it?"

All the Water Creatures kept quiet.

Then Mvu cried, giving a stern look to each one of them in turn, "Come to my cave when the Moon is in the sky and we will settle this."

Now, dear Brothers and Sisters, all the Water Creatures were very afraid, because they knew that Mvu understood many secrets. He would undoubtedly be able to find Ntagi's precious Amulet using his knowledge of Ancient Magic.

When the silver Moon was shining high in the sky, Ntagi, Crab, Minnow, Catfish, Lake Salmon, Turtle and shy Eel swam to Mvu's cave.

As they entered the cave, Rockfish began to beat a slow rhythm on his drum.

Ntagi and the Water Creatures swam towards Mvu the River King, who had a great golden bowl set on the rock before him. Mvu turned his tail three times above the rim of the bowl, thus causing the Ancient Magic to secretly start working. Then he commanded them all, "Swim three times around this bowl."

Ntagi, Crab, Minnow, who was trembling a little, Catfish, Lake Salmon, Turtle and Eel did as he asked.

Then Mvu looked carefully at each of them and saw that tears were streaming down *Minnow's* face.

Mvu pointed a golden fin at tiny Minnow.

"The Ancient Magic has revealed that *you* took the precious Amulet! Go and fetch it quickly and give it back to Ntagi immediately!"

Poor Minnow was so ashamed and humbly begged forgiveness.

"I hoped that the precious Amulet would make me more important," he sobbed.

And that is why, Dear Ones, even to this day, little Minnows get chased away by all the other Water Creatures.

The Beautiful Bird

A story from Swaziland

Hear my tale and come closer.

Long, long ago, when there was still magic in the World, there lived a cunning Father and a lazy Mother.

They had two children, a boy called Tako and a girl called Tifi. They belonged, dear Brothers and Sisters, to a certain tribe who were farmers and grew crops such as maize and groundnuts. They had no cattle.

Now, every morning the Father and the Mother would take down the hoes and the rakes, and send Tako and Tifi out to work in the fields. The children would toil all day in the hot sun, clearing the land and planting.

Then Tako would fill the calabashes with water and Tifi would pick maize, nuts and vegetables, and tired and hungry, they would return to the village for the evening meal.

But instead of giving Tako and Tifi good food to eat, the cunning Father told the lazy Mother to leave them just the scraps that were left over and not to waste good food on the children. And so poor Tako and Tifi got thinner and thinner, whilst their parents became plumper and lazier.

Now this unhappy situation went on for a long time, until one day when Tako said to Tifi, "I cannot work today because my hands are too sore to hold the hoe."

And Tifi said, "I cannot plant the seeds today. My back is too painful when I stoop down."

The two children sat down on the ground and began to cry.

As their hot tears splashed on to the ground, a Beautiful Bird flew down from the sky above and said, "Do not cry, my children. Tell me what is wrong."

Tako said, "We are weak with hunger and cannot work."

"Our parents will be very angry if we do not take maize, nuts, vegetables and water for their evening meal," cried Tifi.

Then the Beautiful Bird turned its lovely golden head and spread its brilliant blue and jewel-red wings, and gently blew a cloud of magic dust over those two helpless ones ... so that they fell into a deep sleep.

Now, when Tako and Tifi woke up they found themselves in a clean and comfortable hut, which would have been fit for a Chief to live in.

The sleeping mats were of the finest woven palm grasses and the wooden neck-rests were beautifully carved.

There were the softest animal skins to keep them warm at night, and clothes sewn from colourful cloths for them to wear during the day.

Two large calabashes there were.

One full with porridge and one full of milk.

Also three woven baskets.

One full of nuts, one full of wheat and one full of maize.

Tako and Tifi were very surprised but also very happy to find themselves in this comfortable place. They thought lovingly of the Beautiful Bird who had brought them here, and said to each other, "Now we shall be happy."

And as the days passed by Tako and Tifi grew strong and happy.

Whenever they took milk or porridge to eat, the calabashes immediately and, as if by magic, filled up again!

And if Tako and Tifi used wheat for flatbread, or maize and nuts for cooking, the woven baskets would fill instantly ... as if by magic.

But one day the calabashes did *not* fill themselves as they had always done before. The children looked at each other and said, "We are now grown and ready to work in the world. Let us leave here and return to the village."

Now, when the Father, who was no longer cunning, and the Mother, who was lazy no more, saw a handsome young man and a lovely young woman coming to their old hut they were overjoyed.

They ran with open arms, crying, "Welcome! We are ashamed that we treated you so badly. Please forgive us for not being a good Father and a kind Mother. We have been so lonely without you and we have learnt our lesson."

And so saying, they fell to their knees, whilst tears of remorse ran down their old, thin faces.

You see, Dear Ones, they had had to do all the work in the fields by themselves. And they had found it very, very hard.

Of course Tako and Tifi forgot all the old unhappy times and tenderly embraced the Father and Mother. And they all lived happily together ever after.

A man who suffers much knows much: every day brings

him new wisdom.

Ewe

The rain does not all fall on one roof.

Ewe

Dilemma Tales

Two tales from Liberia

Who did the biggest stunt?

One man shot through a rock and killed an elephant.

Another followed the shot, butchered the elephant and carried it back through the hole.

The third picked a louse from his head, skinned it, and sewed up the elephant in the louse's skin.

Who did the biggest stunt?

Who had the most power?

Three travellers came to a wide river.

One said he could walk across it with his magic sandals.

Another said he could cut the waters with his magic cutlass and walk across.

The third said that this was too much trouble and that he had a magic thread on which all could cross the river.

Who had the most power?

A tale from Uganda

Who owned the house?

Lion and Bushbuck built the same house.

Each worked on alternate days.

Each claimed it as his own when it was finished.

Who owned the house?

The Tale of Mr Little-Hare

From Zambia

Mr Little-Hare and the Guinea Fowl, dear Brothers and Sisters, were friends.

One day Mr Little-Hare made a crate, climbed inside, and said to the Guinea Fowl, "My friends, won't you pick me up?"

All the Guinea Fowl gathered round to try but none of them could pick him up.

So Mr Little-Hare came out and invited the Guinea Fowl to go into the crate. And indeed all the Guinea Fowl got in.

Then Mr Little-Hare quickly tied up the entrance so that the Guinea Fowl were secure inside, and picked the crate up.

The Guinea Fowl, slightly alarmed, said, "Please put us down!"

And Mr Little-Hare answered, "No, because a certain person wants you."

When they heard that, the Guinea Fowl cried bitterly.

Mean Mr Little-Hare carried the crate to the outskirts of the village, searching for Leopard. When he found Leopard he said, "I want to be your friend. Let us go and eat together."

Naturally, Leopard agreed, so Mr Little-Hare opened the crate to reveal the terrified Guinea Fowl.

Mr Little-Hare and Leopard took the Guinea Fowl …

And cooked them …

And ate them with relish!

That, dear Brothers and Sisters, is how Mr Little-Hare betrayed his friends, the Guinea Fowl.

The Garden

A story from Tanzania

When Earth was young, dear Brothers and Sisters, Man and all the Animals that had ever been created lived together in peace and harmony in the Garden.

All was well for many moons, until a time when some of the Animals grew restless.

"I want to be free to eat from the taller trees," said Giraffe.

"I want to be King of the Jungle," said Lion.

"I want to gallop across greener grasslands," said Zebra.

"I want to discover what is beyond our Garden," said Elephant.

"I want to live by myself," said Rhinoceros.

And even Ostrich, normally so thoughtful and quiet, said, "I want to experience Life."

Then Lizard and Monkey and Hyena and Antelope and Leopard and Wildebeest and all the other Animals agreed that they also wanted to leave the Garden and travel out into places far away to see what they could see.

Man decreed that those Animals that were restless and curious about what lay beyond should leave the Garden.

"Go in peace," Man commanded, "and remember to always worship your Creator."

All the Animals then left the Garden, except for Cow, Goat and Dog who all wished to stay and serve Man.

The Quick-thinking Hyena

A tale from Senegal

Once, long ago, Hyena, who was very hungry because he had not eaten a proper meal for many days, stopped to watch a Man who was butchering two goats and a plump chicken.

"Please give me a little meat or a bone," begged Hyena in a pitiable voice.

"Yes, I will," replied the Man, "*if* you can count to ten without saying the number one."

Hyena sat down to think for a while and then said, "Look at the two goats and the chicken that you are cutting up. Together they have ten feet."

Hyena was right!

He had counted to ten without saying the number one.

The Man laughed and gave Hyena a piece of meat ... *and* a bone.

Quick thinking can be very useful!

The Crocodile and the Monkey

A folk tale from Kenya

Now listen to this story, dear Brothers and Sisters.

Crocodile asked Monkey to visit him.

Monkey asked Crocodile, "How shall I reach your home when I do not know how to swim?"

Crocodile smiled and told Monkey to jump on his back.

On the way Crocodile felt hungry and asked Monkey:

"Can you give me your heart because I am feeling hungry?"

Monkey thought for a short while and then told Crocodile:

"This is what we are going to do. We are going to go back, because when we become friendly with someone, we Monkeys leave our hearts at home."

Then Monkey added, "I am very weak and cannot be eaten. We will go back and I will get you my heart."

Crocodile agreed with the plan and when they reached the shore, Monkey climbed into a mango tree and picked a mango. He threw it down to Crocodile, calling:

"There is my heart."

Crocodile dived into the water and never troubled Monkey again.

The Lord-of-the-Rain's Daughter

A Bantu tale from East Africa

Gather round for this story that I am going to tell you.

Draw closer.

Long, long ago in a certain village there lived a handsome young man, who, although he was truly the son of a Chief, had been brought up by a wise old woman who had taught him many secrets.

One day, the young man said, "It is time for me to marry. I have decided to take for my wife the beautiful daughter of the Lord-of-the-Rain."

So saying, he set out on his journey.

He had not gone very far when a lovely Sun-Bird flew down and settled on a branch which was hanging over his path. The young man reached up to take the bird into his hand, but it flew quickly away and kept just ahead of him for the rest of the day.

The Sun-Bird seemed to be leading the young man on and yes, indeed, Brothers and Sisters, as the day ended, the bird took him to a hut in the middle of the forest.

Here a woman came out and greeted him in the traditional way. She said, "So you have come."

She gave the young man food and water and asked him where he was going.

"I am going to ask the Lord-of-the-Rain for his daughter's hand in marriage."

"Well, we shall see," said the woman. "Meanwhile, please fetch some water."

"Gladly," said he.

The young man fetched several calabashes of water, then he brought wood for the fire. He herded the goats into the pen for the night and milked the cow, before taking its sweet milk to the woman in the hut.

"You have done well," she said.

The next morning, the young man set out on his journey again, but not before the woman had taken a feather from the Sun-Bird's tail and given it to him.

"Tuck this feather in your hair," she said. "It will guide you aright on your journey." And she waved him farewell.

The young man went on and came to a place where the pathway forked one way and another way. The feather fluttered in his hair, and he said, "Feather, feather, what must I do?"

And the feather told him which way to go.

He came to a wide river with rushing water. Again the feather fluttered in his hair and the young man said, "Feather, feather, what must I do?"

And the feather showed him a bridge made of spider-rope so that he could go safely across.

The young man went on and came to a range of steep mountains. Again the feather fluttered in his hair and the young man said, "Feather, feather, what must I do?"

And the feather showed him how to pass through the mountains as if they had been clouds.

At last the young man came to the place where the Lord-of-the-Rain lived. He entered the village and sat down with his arms folded around his knees. He sat like that to show that he had come courting.

Then the people asked the young man many questions. He gave the proper replies and told them that he wished to marry the beautiful daughter of the Lord-of-the-Rain.

Then the Lord-of-the-Rain said, "We had better see what sort of a young man this is."

The best hut was made ready for him, but before the young man entered, the feather fluttered in his hair and he said, "Feather, feather, what must I do?"

"This is not the hut for you," said the feather.

Then the young man was shown to a ruined hut where the roof had fallen in.

"This is the hut for you," said the feather.

And the young man entered in.

Then a fine sleeping mat was brought. But before he sat down on it the feather fluttered in his hair and the young man said, "Feather, feather, what must I do?"

"This is not the mat for you," said the feather.

And the young man sat on the ground.

Then dishes of food were brought, but before the young man could eat, the feather fluttered in his hair and the young man said, "Feather, feather, what must I do?"

"This is not the food for you," said the feather.

And the young man ate just the simple porridge left in a pot.

All these things were told to the Lord-of-the-Rain, and he told his daughter, who was as good and kind as she was beautiful, to make ready for the following day.

The next day a wedding procession came to where the young man was. He saw before him a lovely bride. She was richly dressed in fine clothes made from the loveliest cloths of gold and silver, with closely worked and ornately embroidered borders. She had beautiful shells and ornaments in her hair, and golden hoops around her neck. From her earlobes hung rings of precious jewels, pearls and golden baubles. She had bangles of silver and gold on both her arms and copper anklets with bells that made music as she walked. All the people gasped as the beautiful bride walked slowly by.

Then the feather fluttered in his hair and the young man said, "Feather, feather, what must I do?"

"This is not the bride for you," said the feather.

Then coming behind the bride was a servant girl dressed in simple clothes. She walked gracefully with her head bowed.

She had no jewellery or ornament in her hair, and no bangles on her arms.

But the feather fluttered and said, "This is the bride for you."

And so the young man reached out to his true bride and claimed her as his wife.

All the other suitors had failed, but *he* had had the feather from the Sun-Bird to guide him aright.

It was *he,* who was as noble as he was handsome, who had won the hand of the daughter of the Lord-of-the-Rain.

So ends our tale.

The Punishment of the Elephants

A tale from the Sudan

Long ago, the Sheikh in a certain region wanted to build a mosque. Since there were no tall trees in that area, the Sheikh sent his sons and seven trusted servants on a journey to find timber. They took twenty-one camels with them.

At last they found the timber needed for the great mosque, loaded it on to their camels and started on their return journey.

They went some distance and then decided to stop and rest. Having unloaded the camels, they took food and water under the shade of some trees, but were suddenly surprised by a herd of elephants, who chased all the camels away.

And so it was that the Sheikh's sons and the seven servants were completely stranded in the wilderness with very little food and water and not a living soul to help them.

The Sheikh's eldest son ordered his younger brother to take some of

the servants to find, subdue and bring back the elephants that had chased the camels away, so they might use them instead of the camels.

Of course the younger brother had to obey, but he and the servants felt very afraid and wondered how they were going to tame those wild animals.

However, as the younger brother stood before the elephants he saw a vision of his father giving his blessing and in a truly marvellous way he was then able to subdue and control seven elephants. When asked, the seven huge elephants willingly followed the brother and his servants back to the camp and stood patiently whilst the timber was loaded on to their backs.

Then the party started on the homeward journey.

Wherever the Sheikh's sons stopped to rest, people from different tribes gathered around to see the miracle of the tamed elephants loaded with timber. Even people living in remote tribes on the sides of the great River Nile heard about the miracle and hurried to see for themselves.

Yet when the brothers arrived at their father's dwelling, the Sheikh rebuked them severely for performing such a miracle and drawing attention to themselves.

In his defence, the younger son told his father that, as he had approached the elephants to subdue them, he saw a vision of his father the Sheikh standing in front of them, and he took this to be a sign of his father's approval and blessing for what he was about to do.

The Sheikh couldn't argue with this and welcomed his sons into his dwelling. Then there was great rejoicing and the elephants were unloaded and given food and water.

One of the elephants drank more water than it could hold. It drank and drank until it burst at the foot of a nearby mountain.

Ever since that day, dear Brothers and Sisters, that mountain has been known as Elephant's Mountain and the Sheikh has been called the Punisher of the Elephants.

Elephant, Hippopotamus and Clever Tortoise

A tale from Zaire

I have a tale to tell. Gather round!

One day Tortoise was quietly sunning himself and minding his own business when Elephant came trumpeting along the path in a very important sort of a way.

"Out of my way, Tortoise," he bellowed. "I am so big and strong that if I step on you I will crush you."

Tortoise did not care to move from his sunny patch and so Elephant stepped on him! But thankfully Tortoise's beautiful hard shell did not break.

"Ha ha," said Tortoise. "You see that I am as strong as *you* are."

"Harrumph," replied Elephant, feeling ever-so-slightly put out. "Let's have a tug-of-war to decide who is stronger."

Tortoise and Elephant decided to meet the very next morning for the contest.

Clever Tortoise thought quickly. "Ha ha," he laughed to himself. "I know what I shall do."

Indeed he had thought up a very clever plan, Dear Ones, as you shall hear.

Next day, before the sun rose in the sky, Tortoise met Hippopotamus, who was on his way back to the river after eating sweet grasses all night long.

"Greetings, Hippopotamus. I trust that you are well," Tortoise said, in a friendly sort of a way. "I have decided that I am just as strong as you are and that we should have a tug-of-war contest to prove this."

Hippopotamus laughed at the thought that little Tortoise might be as strong as he, Mr Superbly Strong in Land and in Water Hippopotamus!

"I agree to the challenge," said Hippopotamus, in a good-natured sort of a way.

Tortoise instructed Hippopotamus to hold one end of a long rope in his mouth, and when Tortoise shouted *Hey!* Hippopotamus should pull hard.

Then Tortoise ran up the hill and down the other side. Elephant was waiting, and Tortoise instructed him to hold the other end of the long rope in his mouth and pull hard when Tortoise shouted *Hey!*

Tortoise hurried to his position on the hill. Here he could not be seen by Hippopotamus or Elephant. Then in a loud voice he shouted "*Hey!*" and the Tug-of-War began.

Elephant and Hippopotamus pulled at the rope with all their might and main.

They tugged and they struggled and they hauled at that rope with all their best efforts.

But of course they were of equal strength.

Then Elephant puffed, "Tortoise, you are just as strong as I am."

And Hippopotamus huffed, "Tortoise, you are just as strong as I am."

And clever Tortoise just laughed and smiled an innocent smile!

The Lovely Ten

A story from Mali

Once, dear Brothers and Sisters, in the land of Segou, there was a rich and powerful King who desired, more than anything else, the beautiful country that lay beyond his boundaries. He decided to seek out the wisest counsel in the land to learn how he could capture that land and make it his own.

In order to find the Wisest of All Men in Segou, the King devised a test for all those cowrie-shell tossers, sand drawers, pebble throwers and seers. He took a huge black bowl, and in it placed a white rooster under a black cloth and a tortoise under a white calabash. Many clever men tried to guess what was in the bowl but none had the right answer.

Then a very old man, who was known to be a wise seer, came forward and correctly guessed what was in the bowl. The King was very pleased that his test had worked and invited the old man to dine with him.

The King said, "Wise man, I want you to tell me how my army can capture the beautiful land lying next to our kingdom and seize King Samanyana Basi."

The old seer considered for a while and then said, "King Samanyana Basi will never be taken, unless you can get me the first handful of food from his evening meal and the old sandals from his feet."

The King called all his trusted followers, and asked them to come up with a plan to get these things, but none of them were successful.

Finally, the most beautiful woman in Segou — indeed the loveliest woman that had ever been seen in those parts — came to the King and said that she was willing to help. Her name was Ten.

Ten knelt in front of the King and said, "This whole country, its trees, its animals and its people, from the little river far to the South, to the great river far to the North, belongs to you. If something is bothering you, it is we who must correct it. If you will allow me, I think I will be able to solve your problem."

For besides being the most beautiful of all women, Ten was also very crafty and knew every secret for entering men's hearts and playing with their minds.

The King nodded his head in approval, saying, "And what do you want me to give you?"

Ten said in her sweet voice, "Before I go, I want the best jewellery brought to me. Also gold, silver, precious stones, cowrie shells, the most beautiful and elegant cloth and the finest blankets made in Masina. In addition, I want you to call your Master Brewers to prepare their best beer and wine. When they have finished I will treat it with spices. Once a man has drunk the beer that I shall prepare, he will no longer be a man. He will lose his reason and I shall be able to do what I want with him. I will go to King Samanyana Basi and he will drink his own downfall."

When everything was ready, the King gave Ten his fastest canoe, which was well over thirty feet long, sleek and shiny, and it cut through the water like a boa. Also the King sent her his four best Somono fishermen, the champion canoe men of the Niger River. These four young giants, arms like tree trunks, necks and shoulders like bulls, seized their great bamboo poles and sent the canoe, laden with the beautiful Ten and her riches, shooting upstream. And even when the river deepened, they took their paddles and without losing a stroke, made the canoe fly against the current.

Ten stretched out on the tapestries in the open cabin. She saw all the birds, fish and creatures of the open river. In turn, the crocodiles, the hippos, the great Niger perch, the fierce dogfish and even the river terns sang their praises to the beautiful Ten as she glided by.

Finally, as the sun was setting, the canoe was brought to rest on the shores of King Samanyana Basi's land. The women who had come down to the river to get water, those who were there to bathe, those who were there washing clothes, every one of them stood transfixed.

They could not move their eyes from Ten.

Some said that she was the daughter of a great King and some said that she was a beautiful princess on her way to marry a powerful prince. Still others said that it was their own King Samanyana Basi who had called her to him.

Rumours flew.

Speculation grew.

But Ten did not even set foot on the beach. She just stayed quietly in her canoe.

At last, news about the beautiful Ten reached the King's ears. The King was very curious and a little suspicious, but he sent messengers to bring Ten to his hall. And Ten, radiant with jewellery and fabulous cloth, swept into the hall and knelt in front of King Samanyana Basi.

Following custom, a large gourdful of millet beer was given to Ten so that she could slake her thirst. She drank it down as if it was water. They filled her gourd again and she drank this second beer down more quickly than the first.

The King was amazed and said, "You'd better not drink any more of our beer like that if you want to stay on your feet!"

"What?" Ten replied. "Was *that* your beer? Why, in my country that is what we give our children to drink. That is why I drank it down so quickly. You certainly must know that it's not very strong and surely you wouldn't call it a man's drink!"

"Well," said some of the people in the hall, "this is getting interesting. As our ancestors have said, if a woman goes ahead and swallows a turtle, a man must swallow a lizard."

And everyone fell silent, waiting for King Samanyana Basi to speak. Ten had sprung her trap well, and the King's pride was cut by her quick tongue.

At last he asked, "Who knows how to make the drink *you* call beer?"

"I do," said the lovely Ten, "and I happen to have a sample of real beer and some aged honey wine in my canoe. Let them be brought to you and you can try them."

The servants brought up two great jugs. King Samanyana Basi filled his gourd with Ten's beer and drank it down. Although he remained aloof he was secretly amazed at the sweetness and spiciness of the drink.

Then he filled his calabash with the honey wine and drank that down too! When he had emptied his cup for the third time, he exclaimed with pleasure and Ten knew that he was now defenceless against her charms.

The King then commanded Ten to eat the evening meal with him and Ten laughingly agreed, overwhelming the King with her dazzling beauty and sparkling eyes, which seemed to the King to be full of promise!

A marvellous meal of fragrant rice with a rich meat sauce was prepared, and Ten sat close to King Samanyana Basi. As the King reached into his bowl to bring the first handful of rice and meat to his mouth, Ten reached her hand forward, as if to serve herself, and knocked the food from the King's hand.

"Oh!" she cried. "How terrible! I am so clumsy. I am so stupid. I have knocked the food right out of your hand on to the floor!"

"Don't worry about that," reassured the King. "We have plenty more food in the bowl."

And whilst the King took more rice and meat, Ten reached down and wrapped the spilled food in a cloth. Then she filled the King's gourd and slipped in a strong sleeping potion, so that before long, King Samanyana Basi fell into a deep sleep.

Ten wrapped her robes around herself, and pulled the sandals from the King's feet and his hat from his head. And for good measure, she also took the amulets that hung around his neck. Then she ran down to the beach where the men and her canoe were waiting.

The canoe flew downstream like a sliver of moonlight on the black water. At last, as dawn was breaking, they arrived back in Segou. Ten leaped out and ran with all her prizes to the King, who praised her for her cleverness.

Then the old seer worked over the objects that she had brought and at last discovered the potions that would defeat King Samanyana Basi's magic charms.

The King of Segou sent in his armies, and after only one day of siege they captured King Samanyana Basi and scattered his soldiers and broke down all the defences in that land.

Thus the King's wish came true and his territory was increased.

So there you hear of the deeds of Ten, dear Brothers and Sisters. By her beauty and her wiles, she helped build the empire of one King and destroy that of another. A woman may be beautiful, but she may also be cunning. What is honey to one man may be poison to another.

Jackal and Little Bush Pig

A story from North Africa

Gather round and listen to this story about boastful Jackal and modest Little Bush Pig.

"I have as many tricks as there are stars in the sky," boasted Jackal.

"Oh, I have just one trick," replied Little Bush Pig.

Then Little Bush Pig made a hole in the brush fence that surrounded the farmer's garden and climbed through. Jackal, who was quite thin because he had not eaten for days, was just able to squeeze in after him.

Jackal and Little Bush Pig had the most wonderful feast in that garden and ate and ate until their stomachs were full.

Then it was time to leave.

Jackal was now so round and fat that, try as he might, he could not follow Little Bush Pig and squeeze back through the hole in the brush fence.

"Help me, help me, Little Bush Pig," he panted.

"I would if I could," said Little Bush Pig, who was safely on the other side. "But I had only one trick, which was to get us *into* the garden. Use one of your many tricks to get yourself *out*! But be quick about it, because I can hear the farmer coming."

And the Little Bush Pig, feeling just ever-so-slightly smug, trotted home.

Meanwhile Jackal could do nothing to help himself. There was no escape from the farmer!

Then that farmer, who was angry that his garden had been raided and ruined, beat Jackal roundly and soundly with a big stick.

And if you listen hard you can still hear Jackal, no longer quite so boastful, howling all night long!

Ninety-nine lies may help you, but the hundredth will give you away.

Hausa

The Quarrel Between Earth and Sky

A story from Nigeria

Long, long ago, dear Brothers and Sisters, Earth and Sky had a quarrel and Sky withheld rain for seven years. The crops withered and the hoes broke on the stony Earth.

At last Vulture was sent to plead with Sky, to soften his heart with a song of the suffering of the men of Earth.

Far away in the Sky, Vulture sang for mercy.

At last Sky was moved to pity, and he gave Vulture rain wrapped in leaves of coco-yam.

But as Vulture flew home his talons pierced the leaves and rain fell down on Earth as it had never fallen before.

Vulture was so wet from the torrential rainfall that he decided not to return to deliver his message, but instead flew on to a distant land where he had espied a fire.

When he got there he found that the fire had been lit by a man making a sacrifice in gratitude for the rain.

Vulture warmed and dried himself by the fire and feasted on the entrails of the sacrificed animal.

Infinite boiling will soften the stone.

Konkomba

Father, Son and Donkey

A tale from Ghana

Gather round and listen to my story …

A man, who had a son, farmed yams and guinea corn.

One day the man sold his guinea corn for a good price at the market. He saved some of the money and with the rest he bought a donkey. Then the hot season came and they prepared to store away the yams.

When they had harvested all the crops for that year, the man told his son that he was going to teach him about the world.

"Harness the donkey and load up everything that we need for a journey," he said to his son, "and we will set off."

They had only gone a short distance with the man riding the donkey and his son walking along beside him, when they came across a group of people.

The people pointed at the man and said to each other, "See that foolish man, riding on the donkey whilst his son walks on the hot ground. Father, you are foolish and hopeless!"

And in that way, they continued to insult the man, who kept quiet but said to his son, "Did you hear what they said?"

And the son said that he had.

After they had gone a little further, the man got down from the donkey and told his son to ride whilst he walked. Then they met some women coming the other way.

"See that useless boy. He looks so strong and yet he is riding the donkey and his father is walking on the hot ground." And they swore at him.

The father said, "My son, did you hear?"

And the son said that he had heard.

A little further on, the son got off the donkey and father and son walked one on each side of the good little donkey.

Soon they met people from another village who said, "See that useless man and his son? Neither of them has sense. Why would you have a donkey and yet still walk on the hot ground?"

And the father again said to his son, "Did you hear what they were saying?" But this time he added, "That is the world!"

And he told his son to always do what he thought was right, and to continue doing it even when he was criticised by the whole world.

Trickster Hare and the Water Hole

A Bantu tale from West Africa

Let me tell you a story! If it pleases you, *you* shall tell *me* a tale!

Long, long ago, dear Brothers and Sisters, in a certain time, there was a Great Drought across the land. The mighty rivers dried up and the Earth was parched and brown.

All the Animals began to complain because they could no longer find sweet cool Water to drink.

At last Lion, who was their wise and clever King, called all the Animals to a gathering down at a dried-up water hole. Only Hare, who said that he was too busy, was absent.

Lion ordered all the Animals in turn to stamp hard in the sand, to see if they could force Water to flow up from the underground streams that were in that area.

Elephant, so strong, went first.

He stamped each of his four huge heavy feet, but only a cloud of sandy dust flew up.

Next came Rhinoceros, bad tempered because he was so thirsty.

He dug over every part of that dried-up water hole with his horn, but no water flowed up.

Then it was Wildebeest's turn. He, who was so hardworking.

He used his hooves to stamp and dig but still no water flowed up.

And in turn, Lion ordered Gazelle and Goat, Hyena and Bushbuck, Leopard and Monkey to go down on to the dry riverbed to see if they could make Water flow.

But only clouds of dry sand blew up!

King Lion called for Hare to take his turn but, as we know, Hare was busy with other things!

"May I have a try?" asked little Tortoise.

All the other animals laughed. If *they*, the big important Animals, could not make Water flow up, how did little Tortoise think that *he* could succeed?

But kindly King Lion told little Tortoise to climb down into the dry water hole and try to make Water flow.

So, Dear Ones, imagine the surprise when, just as the sun was setting, little Tortoise, with his steady scratching and poking and bumping and thumping, made Water flow up.

And the water hole filled with sweet cool water.

The large Animals all cheered and congratulated little Tortoise, and King Lion told little Tortoise to take the first drink of Water.

Then King Lion called for silence.

"All you Animals have done well but especially *you* little Tortoise! Only Hare disobeyed me and refused to help us make Water flow. I have decided that he shall not be allowed to drink the sweet cool Water at this hole."

It was agreed that the large Animals would take it in turn to guard the water hole.

Elephant took the first turn.

As Moon rode high in the sky and all was quiet and peaceful, Hare strolled up to the water hole with two calabashes. One was very large and the other very small.

Said Elephant, "You did not help make Water flow up. *You* will not drink here."

Hare replied, "I have something sweeter than Water here. Will you try my delicious honey?"

Then Elephant, tempted by the thought of honey, put his trunk into the small calabash and got it stuck! While he was trying to free himself from the sticky pot, Hare quickly filled up the larger calabash from the water hole, and hopped happily away.

The next day, Rhinoceros guarded the water hole.

As Moon rose high in the sky and all was quiet and peaceful, Hare strolled up to the water hole with his two calabashes. One was very large and the other was very small.

Said Rhinoceros, "You did not help Water flow up, so *you* will not drink here."

The Trickster Hare replied, "I have something that is sweeter than Water here. Will you try my delicious honey?"

Then Rhinoceros, who could not resist the thought of sweet honey, put his horn into the small calabash and yes, it stuck fast in the sticky pot!

Meanwhile Hare dipped his large calabash into the cool Water and filled it to the brim. Then he hopped merrily away.

On the third day, Wildebeest stood guard over the water hole. However, he too was tricked by Hare and finished with the sticky pot stuck fast on his *nose*!

All the large Animals took a turn in guarding the water hole, and Hare tricked every one of them.

At last Lion called a gathering to see how Hare should be properly punished.

But first little Tortoise spoke up. "May I have a turn at guarding the water hole?" he said.

All the large Animals laughed. Did little Tortoise think *he* would succeed where *they* had all failed?

But Lion agreed that little Tortoise should take his turn.

That night, as Moon rose high in the sky and all was peaceful and quiet, Hare strolled up to the water hole with his two calabashes. One was very large and the other was very small, and, as you know, Dear Ones, full of sweet and tempting honey.

Now little Tortoise, so clever and cunning, had taken the trouble to paint sticky sap from the gum tree all over his shell. Then he had waited in the Water for Hare to come along.

Hare thought he had the water hole to himself that night, and stepped right into the Water to take a bath.

Imagine his surprise when first one foot was stuck fast on little Tortoise's sticky back. Then the other hind foot. And then his two front paws!

Hare was caught fast at last!

Meanwhile clever little Tortoise slowly climbed out of the water hole with Hare stuck fast on his back. He made his way carefully to King Lion.

"Oh, Hare," said Lion in his royal voice, "you have been a very bad Animal and deserve punishment."

Then Honey Bee buzzed up, and complained to Lion that Hare had been stealing his honey.

"Go and fetch all the Honey Bees," commanded Lion.

Now maybe *you* can guess how Lion intended to punish Hare?

The swarm of Honey Bees surrounded Hare, who had wriggled free from little Tortoise's shell, and, at a sign from Lion, they flew in their busy, buzzy way all around Hare's floppy ears! Then Hare began to run ...

and run ...

and run ...

The Honey Bees swarmed after him and drove him far, far away.

The Animals, and especially little Tortoise, who was now called the Clever One, were never troubled by Hare's naughty tricks again.

Well, not in those parts anyway!

The Toad and the Frog

A tale in the Gbaya, Cameroon tradition

My children, listen to the tale that I am going to tell.

It is a tale of my fathers.

My father told it to me and I heard it.

I now tell it to you.

A beautiful young girl had two suitors who both wanted to marry her.

One was handsome Frog; the other was ugly Toad.

Frog had a lovely clear skin but was lazy.

Toad was indeed ugly but was the very best of hunters.

The parents gave their lovely daughter to handsome Frog, since they were bewitched by his looks.

Then there was a great burning of the grass and every time the hunters went hunting, they returned empty-handed.

The people were hungry.

But beneath his ugly skin, Toad was a clever and a skilled hunter. He trapped and killed a bull elephant.

He told the other hunters to help him pull the elephant back to the village and he would give them some of the butchered meat as a reward.

So they fastened bush ropes around the elephant and dragged the animal back to Toad's hut, passing right by the girl's parents' house.

The mother and father fled inside and closed the door. They had refused to give their daughter to Toad because he was ugly. And now he had killed an elephant!

They were embarrassed and ashamed that they had wrongly judged Toad.

Goodness isn't in the skin.

If you have wisdom and carefulness, then you are good.

If you are handsome, but your conduct is bad, then *you* are bad.

So, this is the tale my father told me, and now my children can tell it after me.

A weak person goes where he is smiled at.

Herero

Old Tinderbox (The first bringer of fire to Earth)

A Bushman tale from South Africa

In the beginning, Praying Mantis the insect was King of the early people.

One day, Mantis' attention was drawn to Ostrich, whose food always smelt so good. Mantis crept close to Ostrich whilst he was eating. He saw for the first time Ostrich roasting food on a fire. When Ostrich had finished eating, he carefully picked up the fire and tucked it deep into the pit under his wing.

Mantis immediately realised the advantages of fire and wondered how he could get it from Ostrich. For days he went about scheming in his mind. Already the vision of the fire was teaching him to think.

At last he hit on a plan.

Mantis said to Ostrich, "I have found a tree with the most wonderful fruit on it. Come with me and I will show you."

Ostrich followed Mantis out into the desert to a certain tree, on which grew the lovely yellow wild plums that elephants, to this day, walk thousands of miles in the rainy season to savour. Ostrich began eating at once.

Mantis said, "Pick your fruit with more care! Eat higher up! The tastiest ones are at the top." Ostrich reached higher and higher. But still Mantis urged, "That's not high enough! Look at that big yellow one up there!"

Ostrich was excited and stood on tiptoe, opening wide his wings to balance himself. At that instant Mantis snatched some of the fire from underneath Ostrich's wing.

Before that moment Ostrich could fly. Afterwards Ostrich never flew again, lest in opening his wings he should lose the little fire he had left.

And that is how Mantis stole fire and was known as "Old Tinderbox."

64

Three Short Tales from Malawi

The Little People

In the Old Days, the Batwa, or Little People, were very sensitive about their size.

They were so little that they could move through the bush without being seen and they could creep up on game without being spotted.

But they had big hearts and were also skilled in hunting and bushcraft.

They saw themselves as tall men, as tall as the gum trees that grew in that place.

When they met with strangers in the bush their first question was:

"Where did you see me?"

To which the only acceptable answer was:

"I saw you from far away ..."

The Story of Che Mlanda

Che Mlanda, the little brown bird, was always hopping about, fussing and cheeping.

Do you know how he got such a dull coat?

Well, Dear Ones, when the Great Chief was giving all the birds their coloured feathers, Che Mlanda was too impatient to wait his turn. He hopped up and down, he fussed about and cheeped noisily to attract attention, but then flew off in a huff, before the Great Chief could adorn him with beautiful jewel-coloured feathers.

He might have been bright blue like Kingfisher, or green and red like Bee-eater ... but there he is!

Lazy Rock Rabbit

And do you know, Dear Ones, why Rock Rabbit has no tail?

It is because Rock Rabbit was too lazy to come along to the first gathering when tails were given out!

Sun, Wind and Cloud

An East African story

Listen to this tale, dear Brothers and Sisters, and remember to give thanks to the God of All Living Things.

Once upon a time, Sun and Wind were having a quarrel about which of them was the most powerful.

Sun said, "When *I* get really angry, the whole world will dry up from the heat of my rays."

"Oh ho," said Wind. "When *I* get really angry the whole land will tremble with fear."

Little Cloud was floating by and gently suggested that the quarrel should be settled by a contest.

Then Sun, becoming angry, started to climb into the sky and shine more and more brightly. The brighter Sun shone, the hotter Earth became. And then, getting even more angry, Sun scorched the ground and dried up all the rivers and turned all that had been green, parched and brown.

Then all the Animals said to each other, "We have done wrong. The God of all Living Things is angry with us. We must ask forgiveness and beg for Rain." And they asked Antelope to go swiftly to the God of All Living Things with their urgent plea for Rain.

Sun proudly said to Wind, "You see, my friend. I am so powerful that all the Animals have had to beg the God of All Living Things for help!"

Now Wind, growing angry, took *his* turn to demonstrate his power.

He blew gently on the hunter's fire, out on the grasslands.

Then he grew stronger and blew even harder, so that the sparks jumped from the fire and made new fires across the land.

Then Wind roared more and more and soon fire was spreading through the bushes and trees, and black smoke poured up into the sky!

All the Animals, maddened by fear, ran hither and thither to escape from the scorching fires.

The sky glowed red and orange and billows of smoke filled Little Cloud, whose eyes began to fill with tears.

"Oh, stop, Wind," cried Little Cloud.

But Wind would not listen!

Then Little Cloud began to cry and Rain started to fall on the Earth below.

And as Little Cloud cried harder and harder, Rain flowed in torrents and flooded all the rivers and lakes.

Earth grew green again and Antelope told the Animals that the God of All Living Things had answered their cry for help.

Sun and Wind were ashamed and agreed that Little Cloud was more powerful than either of them.

And to this day, Brothers and Sisters, all the Animals give thanks to the great God of All Living Things for Rain.

The Fisherman and the Ring

A tale from Malawi

Gather round and listen to this story ...

Once upon a time, long ago, there lived a great Chief who was a fine hunter. He had one son whom he loved dearly, and to whom he taught all his hunting skills.

When the son was a young man, he said to his father, "Let me go to the Great Lake. I wish to be a fisherman, and hunt for fish in the waters of the Lake."

And so the Chief agreed, although he was surprised that his son wanted to hunt in water rather than on land.

The son built his hut on the shores of the Lake and set about making his canoe. He chose just the right blue gum tree, and dug out the wood to make a splendid canoe. Then he made fine ropes from sisal grasses, and set about weaving large nets for catching smaller fish. Next he made thick ropes from vines hanging in the tall trees. These he would use to haul the laden nets from the waters. He cut long slender poles and bound hooks, which he carved from fishbone, on to one end. He would use these poles for catching bigger fish.

When all was ready, he placed his nets, ropes and poles in the canoe and set out across the Lake. He caught plenty of fish and became known as a skilled and generous fish hunter. He gave the largest fish in the catch to his father, the Chief. Nobody in his village ever went hungry.

Then famine came to that land and the young fish hunter gave even more fish to the Chief and the people in the village. Every day he paddled far across the water of the Lake to hunt for fish.

One day he hauled in his sisal grass nets and was surprised to see a great Red Fish looking up at him!

The great Red Fish, whose name was Obi, said, "Oh, please, do not kill me."

The young fish hunter was greatly surprised when the Red Fish spoke to him and replied, "Greetings. You are a very beautiful Red Fish. I will let you go back into the waters of the Lake."

And Obi said, "Thank you. I will reward you for your kindness."

Then Obi dropped a ring from his mouth into the young fish hunter's hand.

"This is a magic ring," Obi said. "Whatsoever you wish for will be so."

Greatly surprised, the young fish hunter thanked Obi and put the ring on his finger.

Then he fished and wished for a large catch so he could feed the hungry villagers.

Imagine, Dear Ones, his surprise when his nets were so full of fish that he could hardly haul them in!

Nobody went hungry.

The famine passed, and then news of war came to that area.

The young fish hunter remembered what the magic fish had said, that whatsoever he wished for would be so! And so the young fish hunter wished for protection for his village and for all of that area.

Immediately a range of mountains sprang up so high and so wide that no warring tribes could cross it.

The young fish hunter, his father the Chief, and all the people in the village lived in peace and simple prosperity, and ever after told tales of the wondrous talking fish and the magic ring.

The Proud Horse

A story from Sudan

Long, long ago, dear Brothers and Sisters, when Earth was still young, Horse, who, to tell you truthfully, thought himself the most beautiful of all the Animals, grew dissatisfied.

One day, as he swished his long thick tail, he complained to Giraffe:

"I know I am a surpassingly beautiful Animal, but I wish I had a long neck like *you*, Giraffe. Then I could reach up and eat tasty leaves and fruits from the high branches just as you do."

Another day, as Horse thundered along on his flying hooves, he complained to Antelope:

"I know that I am more beautiful than you, but I wish I could run through the trees as noiselessly as *you*, Antelope. Then Man could not catch me."

And then Horse, proudly tossing his head to make his marvellous mane fly about, saw old Tortoise, and said:

"There is no question about who is the most beautiful between you and I. But I do wish that I could go for long distances without eating and drinking, as *you* do. And then I would not have to stop to drink water and eat grass so often."

Naturally, Dear Ones, the Animals grew tired of proud Horse and his vain wishes, and at last spoke to the Lord God Almighty.

Then it pleased God to create an Animal just as Horse would have it.

And that is how Camels were born!

The Wise Old Father

A story from Zambia

Now listen to my story!

These things happened long, long ago, not in my village and not in your village, but far away on the other side of the mountains.

There was once an Old Father who had only one son, but that son was handsome and good and listened to his father who always gave him wise advice.

One day the Old Father said to his son, "It is time for you to marry. You must travel far to the West until you come to a village where a Chief keeps his beautiful daughter hidden in a hut. It is said that the Chief has been bewitched by a Magical Lizard. No man will marry his daughter until that day when a suitor brings Agu the Magical Lizard down from the top of the Tallest-Palm-Tree-in-the-World, and breaks the spell."

Then the Old Father told his son to accept advice with a humble heart from whomsoever it may come.

The young man walked for many days and at last arrived in the village where the Chief kept his beautiful daughter hidden in a hut. The young man knelt before the Chief and spoke.

"I wish to marry your daughter, O Chief," he declared.

Then the Chief said, "First you must bring Agu the Magical Lizard to me and at last release us all from his evil spell."

And he pointed to the top of a very tall palm tree, said to be the Tallest-Palm-Tree-in-the-World.

There sat old Agu the Magical Lizard!

Just then, Mbe the Mosquito whispered in the young man's ear, and this is what he said:

"Tie a goat to the tree and feed it meat. Also tie a dog to the tree and feed it grass. Do as I say!"

"I will take your advice," said the modest young man, who remembered his Old Father's instruction to listen carefully to advice from whomsoever it may come.

Although, Dear Ones, we have to say that this was rather strange advice, the young man tied the goat to the tree and gave it meat to eat. Then he tied the dog to the tree and gave it grass to eat.

Now Agu the Magical Lizard looked down and shouted out in a commanding voice, "Are you a fool? Everyone knows that the *goat* should be fed grass and the *dog* should be fed the meat!"

But the handsome young man kept his head down and pretended not to hear.

Agu shouted down again, mocking the young man, "You foolish young man! Give the goat grass to eat and give the dog meat to eat!"

The young man remembered the advice Mbe the Mosquito had given him and took no notice of Agu.

Meanwhile Mbe whispered into the young man's ear, "Have a sack ready."

Agu was now irritated to such a degree that he started to come down from that high perch.

That Magical Lizard slithered
    and slid
    and slipped
  and slinked
all the way down to the ground
where he lost his magic!

The young man jumped forward and popped Agu the Magical-Lizard-No-Longer into the sack.

The Chief, with tears of gratitude streaming down his face, praised the young man and joyfully gave his beautiful daughter to him in marriage.

Then the young man took his bride to greet his Wise Old Father.

"Your obedience has brought you a prize beyond measure, my son," said the Old Father with tears of pride and happiness in his eyes.

And so young people should always listen to the Counsel of the Elders.

Tortoise and Baboon Match Tricks

A West African tale

Now long ago, Dear Ones, when all the Animals lived together, there was a time of great hardship.

Fire had blackened and scorched Earth, Rain seldom quenched the ground, and all the Animals had difficulty in finding enough food to eat.

One day Baboon, full of mischief as usual, swung down from the tall trees and addressed Tortoise, who was slowly making his way home.

"You look hungry, old friend. Come and eat with me this very evening."

"Why, thank you, Baboon," said Tortoise politely, although secretly he was very puzzled by Baboon's unexpected invitation.

You see, Baboon was well known for playing annoying pranks on the other Animals. However, because Tortoise was so very hungry he could not resist the thought of a good meal, and agreed to go with Baboon.

"I will go ahead and prepare delicious food for you," chortled Baboon.

Tortoise followed as quickly as he could and arrived even more tired and hungry at Baboon's house.

"Greetings," said Baboon, "you have come at last! Our meal is now ready. All you have to do is climb up to that branch."

And much to poor Tortoise's dismay, Baboon pointed to three steaming pots wedged in the highest branch of the tree.

"But, but ..." stammered Tortoise, "I cannot climb the tree. Please bring the pots down here."

"No, no," said naughty Baboon. "Any guest who eats with me has to climb up into the tree."

Of course, he knew fine well that Tortoise would not be able to climb the tree.

Baboon thought it all an excellent joke, and screamed with laughter as poor Tortoise made his weary way home.

We shall see, we shall see, thought Tortoise to himself.

Well, Dear Ones, nine sun-risings later, clever Tortoise had a plan.

73

"Oh, Baboon, please come and dine with me," he said in a friendly sort of a way.

Baboon was surprised that Tortoise bore him no ill-will after that cruel joke he had played. He even felt just ever-so-slightly ashamed of himself!

"Thank you, Tortoise, I will come," he replied grandly. Secretly he was greedily looking forward to a good dinner.

At the right time, Baboon, who was now very hungry and ready to eat, left his tree, crossed the river and hurried across the parched and blackened earth.

He sniffed the air.

Delicious smells of food roasting and toasting were coming from Tortoise's cook-fire.

"Greetings," said Tortoise, "you have come in time. But first go down to the river and wash off that black soot. You must be clean to eat with me."

Baboon looked down at his hands and feet and saw that they were indeed black from crossing the sooted, scorched earth. Away he went to the river and was quickly back again, more than ready for his food.

"Oh dear me no!" crowed Tortoise. "Look at your hands! Go back to the river and wash them again!"

And once again, and then again, Baboon rushed to the river to wash his hands.

But once again, and then again, he had to cross that black sooty earth to get back to Tortoise's feast. And in so doing blackened his hands and feet with soot *again*.

This washing business went on for some time until Baboon, who was being a little slow in working it all out, realised that each time Tortoise shook his head, he only *pretended* to be just a little bit sorrowful and regretful as he said, yet again, "Oh dear me no! You must be clean to eat with me."

Then Baboon knew that cunning Tortoise had out-tricked him, and he went back to his tree feeling very cross, and hungry!

Tortoise enjoyed the good roasted and toasted food all by himself.

"That will teach you a lesson, my friend!" he chuckled.

Lord of the Jungle

A tale from Nigeria

My story is this.

Once, long ago, Leopard, who because he was the most feared of all the Animals, was Lord of the Jungle.

One morning Leopard told the Animals that he needed a new house. The Animals agreed to help him build one, and Leopard chose a suitable place right in the middle of the jungle.

"Have my new house ready by the time I come back from my hunting trip," he said in a lordly manner. Then Leopard leapt away.

First, Tortoise was called to dig good deep foundations, whilst Elephant tramped amongst the oldest parts of the jungle, uprooting the best and most suitable trees for the frame of the house.

Then Lion measured out the timbers and Antelope dropped them into the post-holes, which Anteater had carefully rounded out.

Hare filled in the walls with wattle and Baboon daubed on clay from the riverbank.

Giraffe and Ostrich together bound the roof-beams in place.

Goat brought bundles of reeds and the Birds wove thatch for the roof.

Then the Animals, who had worked tirelessly all day, stood back and admired the house they had built for Leopard.

"We have built a very good house. Leopard will be happy," they said to each other.

But sadly, dear Brothers and Sisters, when Leopard returned from his hunting trip, he did *not* thank the Animals for all their hard work.

He did *not* admire the house and tell the Animals what good friends they were.

And he did *not* show his gratitude by inviting them to share a meal with him!

Leopard did none of these things.

And the Animals, quite rightly, started to grumble and complain to each other about his bad manners.

Goat was chosen to be the spokesperson and went to Leopard to remind him of his manners.

And do you know what Leopard did?

He gobbled Goat up!

Now all the Animals were very angry and marched together to Leopard's new house. There they found Leopard lying in the sun.

Elephant, who was the most angry of all, trumpeted very loudly and with his tremendous weight crushed the walls of the new house!

Then Giraffe and Ostrich tipped the roof from the support poles.

And Lion snapped and snarled at Leopard, who ran far away from that place to the lonely barren mountainsides ... with his tail well and truly between his legs ...

And there he still lives to this day, without the comfort of friendship with the other Animals.

When all was quiet and calm again, the Animals addressed Elephant, who was highly respected and admired for his strength and courage.

"We all agree that you, Elephant, should now be the Lord of the Jungle."

So that, Dear Ones, is how Elephant became Lord of the Jungle.

Mr Leopard and Little Goat

A story from Mali

One day, long ago, when the Animals lived together in mutual respect and harmony, Little Goat strayed too far from home.

She was enjoying the lush green grasses that were sweet and most delicious, since Rain had recently visited Earth. Each time Little Goat lifted her head from nibbling at a certain patch of grass, she would spy some, even greener and more lush, just a little further away, which she just *had* to try.

And that, Dear Ones, is how Little Goat came to be quite so far from home.

Then Mr Leopard sprang down from a rock and asked crossly, "What are you doing in my bushes, Little Goat?"

Little Goat was afraid when she saw Mr Leopard, but she tried not to show it.

"I have come just so that you can eat me for your dinner," she said prettily.

Well, Mr Leopard laughed when he heard this.

"Then listen to me now," he said, with a slightly sly grin. "You must tell me two true things. If you do not tell me two true things, I will eat you for my dinner!"

Little Goat thought quickly and replied, "Yes, Mr Leopard, I think I can tell you two true things."

Mr Leopard came closer and said, "Speak up then, Little Goat."

And Little Goat said boldly, "One is this. I know that you are not hungry, otherwise you would have eaten me already."

"True," said Mr Leopard, nodding his head.

Little Goat took a deep breath to give herself courage.

"The other thing is this," she said. "When I go back to the village and tell my neighbours that I met Mr Leopard, but that he did *not* eat me, they will not believe me!"

"Also true," agreed Mr Leopard. "I will let you go free, but do not stray this way ever again."

And in future Little Goat stayed close to home.

Tako the Tortoise and Guye the Hornbill

A tale from Ghana

Dear Brothers and Sisters, this is a tale with a sad ending. Now listen!

One day, when the sun was at its highest and all the Animals were resting, Tako the Tortoise made his way to his favourite place beneath the acacia tree. Here it was cool, quiet and shady, and Tako could take his ease at the hottest time of the day.

Suddenly, with a great deal of noise and commotion, Guye the Hornbill landed heavily in the branches of the acacia tree above Tako's head.

When Guye began to practise his song rather too loudly, Tako looked up and said, "Be quiet, Guye, you are disturbing the peace and quiet. What is more, you may attract the attention of a hunter."

Guye looked down at Tako the Tortoise and replied, "O slow one, if a hunter comes, I can fly away faster than the wind. Do not worry about me."

Guye the Hornbill then went on recklessly practising his loud and tuneless song.

Indeed, Dear Ones, a hunter did hear this noise and hurried towards the acacia tree.

He knelt down, took aim, and sent an arrow speeding towards the noisy, careless bird.

Guye fell through the branches and lay dying close to Tako.

The hunter hurried up and put both Hornbill and Tortoise into his bag.

"You see," scolded Tortoise, "I warned you, but you took no notice. Now we are both for the pot."

And dying now, Guye the Hornbill cried, "I am so sorry. My pride and carelessness have brought trouble for both of us."

Let this be a lesson for all who hear the story. One man suffers because of another man's foolishness.

How Hare Got His Split Lip

A Bushman Tale from South Africa

Long ago, before time, dear Brothers and Sisters, Moon sent Hare with a message for the people on Earth.

"Tell the people on Earth," said Moon, "as I in dying am renewed again, so shall you in dying be renewed again."

Hare did not pay attention and got the words wrong.

He told the first men on Earth, "Moon says that unlike him, who in dying is renewed again, you in dying will not be renewed again."

So angry was Moon with Hare for this fatal mistake that he beat him on the mouth and split Hare's lip.

Ever since then, the Bushman had only to look at the hare's lip to be reminded that death was not intended to be the end, and that whosoever would have it so was bearing false witness ...

The Quarrel

An East African story

Long ago, in a time before time, the Animals began to argue about which of them was the most excellent of all.

"I am," said Tortoise, "because I am the Wisest."

"I am," roared Lion, "because I am the most Feared."

"I am," hissed Python, "because I am the most Deadly."

"I am," cried Fish Eagle, "because I can soar the Highest."

"I am," argued Baboon, "because I can travel the Furthest."

"I am," trumpeted Elephant, "because I am the Strongest."

"I am," snorted Horse, "because I am the most Handsome."

"I am," snapped Cheetah, "because I am the Fastest."

"I am," bellowed Hippopotamus, "because I live on Land and in Water."

Porcupine listened to all the Animals arguing about which of them was the most excellent, and at last he spoke up.

"We are all excellent in our different ways. Let us not argue with each other."

And all the Animals stopped quarrelling, and agreed that it was better to live in harmony with each other.

And so, Dear Ones, from that day to this, Porcupine was called Peacemaker.

The Wicked Leopardess and the Clever Sheep

A story from Nigeria

Olulu ofu oge, or should we say ...

Once upon a time, dear Brothers and Sisters, Leopardess was very, very hungry. She had not eaten for days. She was so hungry that she decided to eat the young lambs of her old friend Sheep.

Yes, you are right, dear Brothers and Sisters, this is not what a good old friend should do. But in those days there was a shortage of food.

Leopardess went to Sheep's hut when she knew that Sheep had gone to market and began to search for the young lambs.

She did not know that clever Sheep had hidden her young inside some of the palm-kernels lying on the ground.

At last Leopardess gave up the search and found two stones to crack some of the kernels, so that she could eat before going.

She was so very hungry!

As soon as Leopardess cracked open the first kernel, the nut flew out of the hut into the bush. She was very surprised.

The second nut also flew out of the hut into the bush. Leopardess was amazed.

But when the third nut jumped up and slapped her before flying out into the bush, Leopardess was so frightened that she raced away from the hut and was not seen for a long, long time.

God's Hat

A story from West Africa

On a day long ago, dear Brothers and Sisters, God took a walk across the Earth disguised as a poor old man. He came to a place where four men were hoeing their fields and he decided to have a joke with them. He put on a hat that was red on one side, white on the other, green at the front and black at the back.

As the friends walked back to their village that night, they talked about the poor old man.

"Did you see that poor old man in the white hat walking through the field?" said the first.

"No, it was a red hat," replied the second.

"It was definitely white," stated the first.

"I saw it with my own two eyes! And it was red," argued the second.

"You must be blind!" said the first.

"There's nothing wrong with my eyes! It's you ... you must be drunk," snapped the second.

"You are both blind," chimed in the third. "That man's hat was green."

"What's the matter with you all," shouted the fourth friend. "It was a black hat. Any fool could see that!"

And the four argued back and forth until they had all fallen out with each other and they had become enemies.

And to this very day the strife continues and the descendants of those former friends go on arguing about the colour of the hat.

As for God, He still walks through the fields in disguise, but everybody is too busy arguing to notice Him.

How the Friendship Between Hawk and Fowl Ended

A tale from Ghana

Gather round. A story is coming!

Setu the Hawk and Nmengu the Fowl were very good friends. One day they decided to make talking drums so that they could dance. They went into the bush, cut down a big tree and set about carving the talking drums.

After all the work, Setu the Hawk was very hungry, so he told Nmengu the Fowl to sit in the sun and look after the drums while he went off to eat.

"But," he warned, "when the drums are dry do not beat them. If you beat them before I return there will be trouble between us!" And Setu the Hawk flew away to find food.

Time went by and the drums dried.

Nmengu the Fowl looked at those drums. Then he inspected them to see if they were perfectly dry. He took them up and stroked them. And he gently beat those drums. He could not resist.

Gben-gben-gben

He liked the sound of the drums. And he beat some more.

Faraway Setu the Hawk heard the sound of the drums and became very annoyed. He flew back, staying up very high.

Nmengu the Fowl beat the drums, not knowing that the more he beat …

Gben-gben-gben

… the angrier Setu the Hawk became.

Setu flew very fast past Nmengu. The Fowl thought that the Hawk was happy and he beat the drum even harder.

Setu the Hawk flew lower and lower over Nmengu until he could just reach to give the Fowl's head a hard peck.

Nmengu ran away as fast as he could — and this is how their friendship was spoiled.

Neither Setu the Hawk nor Nmengu the Fowl took the talking drums that they had worked so hard to make. But the village people took those drums and used them for their dancing.

The White Bird

A Hottentot story from South Africa

Once upon a time and long ago, dear Brothers and Sisters, a Hunter went to a place of reeds and flowers and birds singing by the deep water.

He knelt down to fill his calabash with the sweet drinking water.

As he did so he was startled to see, reflected in the shining surface of the water, an enormous White Bird that he had never seen before.

He looked up quickly but the beautiful bird was already flying away over the tops of the trees.

From that moment on, the Hunter's heart was filled with a restless longing to capture the bird.

The Hunter left his cattle.

He left his wife and his children.

He left all the people in his village and went deep into the forest looking for the white bird and then out into the great world beyond.

Yet everywhere he found nothing but rumour of the bird.

At last, when he was a very old man and close to his end, he was told that he would find the bird on a great white mountain in the heart of Africa, far north of his home.

He journeyed for many weeks and at last found the mountain and started climbing it.

He climbed for days until he found himself on the white cap of the mountain.

And still there was no sign of the bird!

Feeling that he had failed in his quest, he threw himself down crying, "Oh! My mother! Oh!"

Then a voice answered him and said, "Look!"

He looked up and saw, in the red sky of an African sunset, a white feather falling slowly towards him.

He held out his hand and grasped it.

With the feather in his hand, he died content as the night fell.

It was the great White Bird. No one knows its name. But one feather from it in the Hunter's hand was enough.

One feather of it on the head of the Chief brought happiness to all his people.

The Seven Bridegrooms

A Nyanja story from Malawi

Draw closer, my children, and let me tell you the tale of the seven Bridegrooms.

Long ago, in the deep dark forests, lived Kholo the Ape and her six sons.

One day Kholo picked up a tiny Black Monkey, a foundling, which had been left at the foot of a great Baobab tree. She took the foundling home and brought it up as her own son. She called him Luka.

Time passed, and then Kholo, who had a cousin with marriageable daughters, called her seven sons to her.

"You are ready to be Bridegrooms. You must travel to the edge of the forest and there you will find your Brides being made ready for you."

Now the six grey Ape brothers were very jealous of Luka. Although Luka was smaller than they were, he was tremendously agile and also very handsome and good-natured. And besides, he had a silky black coat that shone like polished ebony in the sunshine. The Ape brothers felt *very* grey beside him

While the six brothers planned their journey, they secretly plotted some mischief together.

When all was ready, Kholo bade them farewell and told them to look after each other.

The seven Bridegrooms set out and travelled quickly through the thick dense branches of the forest, swinging easily from tree to tree.

Butterfly flew close to Luka and whispered to him, "Be careful! Your brothers are plotting mischief. They are jealous of you and do not want you to be one of the Bridegrooms."

So Luka was careful not to displease his brothers. When they stopped to rest he gathered wild figs for them to eat. Then he brought fresh water from the spring for them all to drink.

Refreshed, they travelled on.

At last the oldest Ape brother said, "I can hear the drums from the village. Our Brides are being made ready and are even now waiting for us. We will rest here tonight and then go to our wedding ceremony in the morning."

But first, Dear Ones, those naughty, mischievous brothers tricked Luka!

Do you know what they did?

They tied him up with vines, then daubed that poor black monkey with sticky sap from a gum tree and then rolled him in the *sand* ... and left him to his fate in the undergrowth ...

In the morning those impudent six brothers strutted into the village where their Brides, six attractive, but not very kind, grey Ape sisters were waiting. They had been preening and preparing for this wedding day for many moons, and fell eagerly into the waiting arms of their Bridegrooms.

There was much drumming, feasting and drinking of palm wine. The six newly-wed couples set about celebrating and making merry. None of them had a care in the world!

But you, Dear Ones, care about what happened to poor Luca!

Now, it so happened that a servant called Nanita, despised by the six grey Ape sisters because she was such a beautiful Black Monkey with a silky coat that shone like polished ebony in the sunshine, was ordered to take calabashes and fetch more water from the river. She was always ordered to do all the most menial tasks.

But Nanita was as good and kind as she was beautiful, and did as she was told. As she made her way to the river, Butterfly, her friend, flew close and whispered, "Your Bridegroom waits for you here."

Nanita was so surprised when Butterfly alighted on a strange, sandy, sticky shape, which turned out to be poor Luka, that she almost dropped the calabashes.

Then she helped Luka to wash all the sap and sand from his long black coat, and Luka, who was once again his handsome self, thanked her.

To tell you the truth, Brothers and Sisters, Luka looked at Nanita and fell instantly in love with her.

"Will you be my Bride?" he asked.

Nanita sighed with happiness and said, "Yes, I *will* be your Bride."

The six Bridegrooms and their Brides and all the wedding guests gasped with amazement when Luka and Nanita returned to the village.

Never had anyone seen such a handsome couple.

Their long black silky coats gleamed like polished ebony and a great happiness shone from their faces.

The six grey Ape brothers were ashamed, just a little, and their Brides were already scolding them for not being as handsome as Luca!

So each one got his just reward.

And as for Luka and Nanita?

Well, those two fortunate Black Monkeys lived happily together for many years after in pine forests on high mountain slopes, far away from the mischief-making grey Apes.

Acknowledgements

As these stories have been passed down in oral tradition over decades, it is impossible to trace their true origins. I have made every effort to trace and contact copyright owners, but apologise for any oversights. I would particularly like to acknowledge material taken from Laurens van der Post's wonderful book, *The Heart of the Hunter*.

I would like to thank the many people who have been hugely supportive. Alex Cargill, the Managing Director of Scottish and Universal Newspapers Ltd, for his enthusiasm, expertise and for referring me to Alison Lowson and Alison Campbell and team. Sarah Bramley for completing the wonderful artwork. I wish her all the success in what I know will be a brilliant career. Tony Spearing for the beautiful cover drawings. Alexander McCall Smith and Lesley Winton for their encouragement and support. Mark Zumbuhl and Kate Boileau for their artistic contributions. Sheila Bell for her speedy typing and Pauline Mickel for her great encouragement. Eva Langlands for her contribution. Anita, Lene and Jenny for their unseen and endless support. Susila Dharma (Britain) for stimulating and nurturing this initiative. And immense admiration for Hamid and Margriet, founder members of the Children's Fund of Malawi and driving forces behind the Chiuta Children's Village. I hope that the money raised from this book helps to make their dreams a reality.

Lastly, my beloved Aziz, for sharing my endeavours. And my four children: Sara, Rosada, Adam and Dominic, who are behind me all the way.

Bibliography

Amabel Williams-Ellis, *The Rain-God's Daughter*
— Trickster Hare and the Water Hole; The Lord-of-the-Rain's Daughter;
The Beautiful Bird
Dorathea Lehmann, *Folk Tales from Zambia*
— The Wise Old Father
Geraldine Elliot, *The Hunter's Cave*
— The Lost Amulet; The Seven Bridegrooms
Hugh Vernon-Jackson, *African Folk Tales*
— Sun, Wind and Cloud; The Hunter, the Egg, the Broom and the Stone;
The Fisherman and the Ring
Jan Knappert, *Fables from Africa*
— The Garden; Elephant, Hippopotamus and Clever Tortoise; The Proud
Horse; Jackal and Little Bush Pig; Mr Leopard and Little Goat; The Quick-
thinking Hyena; The Quarrel; Lord of the Jungle
Kathleen Arnott, *African Myths and Legends*
— Tortoise and Baboon Match Tricks
Laurens van der Post, *The Heart of the Hunter*
— The Basket of Dreams; Old Tinderbox; The Bull and the Woman; How
Hare Got His Split Lip; The White Bird
Peggy Appiah, *The Pineapple Child and other Tales from Ashanti*
— How Wisdom Was Spread; Tako the Tortoise and Guye the Hornbill
Richard M Dorson, *African Folklore*
— The Two Brothers; Dilemma Tales; The Crocodile and the Monkey; The
Tale of Mr Little-Hare; The Punishment of the Elephants; Father, Son and
Donkey; How the Friendship Between Hawk and Fowl Ended
Veronique Tadjo, *Chasing the Sun*

The Children's Fund of Malawi

Scotland **Malawi** Partnership

The Children's Fund of Malawi was set up in 1992 to give children in Malawi a better chance in life. Run by a small group of volunteers in Malawi, the fund provides food, shelter, education and healthcare. All funds raised go directly to projects.

Of the 13 million people living in Malawi, one million are orphaned children. The spread of HIV/Aids, drought, disease and poverty mean children in Malawi live with insecurity. Yet it only costs £4 to feed one child for an entire month. Since 2007 the fund's particular focus has been to raise money for the Chiuta Children's Village in southern Malawi.

By buying this book, you will help build a better future for a child.

The fund is under the umbrella of the Scotland-Malawi Partnership, which was set up in 2004 to help relieve poverty in Malawi. The two countries enjoy a long-standing relationship that stretches back 150 years to the time of David Livingstone. The Partnership involves more than 100 Scottish organisations and individuals helping the Malawian government with their own priorities in education, health, water and sanitation through the funding of sustainable projects.

For more information go to:
    www.childrensfundmalawi.org
    www.scotland-malawipartnership.org